The Night
the Lights Went Out

Anna Perera

illustrated by Carl Pearce

Tamarind

Tamarind

Rana was cleaning her teeth...

when
a strong north
wind tickled
the windows,
rumbled down
the chimney
and...

POP!

Out went all the lights.

"MUM!" Rana turned round and round
in a darkness as wide as the ocean.
"I'm looking for a candle," shouted Mum.

In the darkness
Rana tried to find the door.

Rana opened the door and tiptoed down a wide inky hall.

into a bedroom
as deep as
a cave.
Three steps and
she fell on the bed.
"Got you!" Rana
held Fluffy Bear
tight.

Then Dad was there,
folding his warm hands
round hers.
"Everything's fine,"
he said. "Come on."

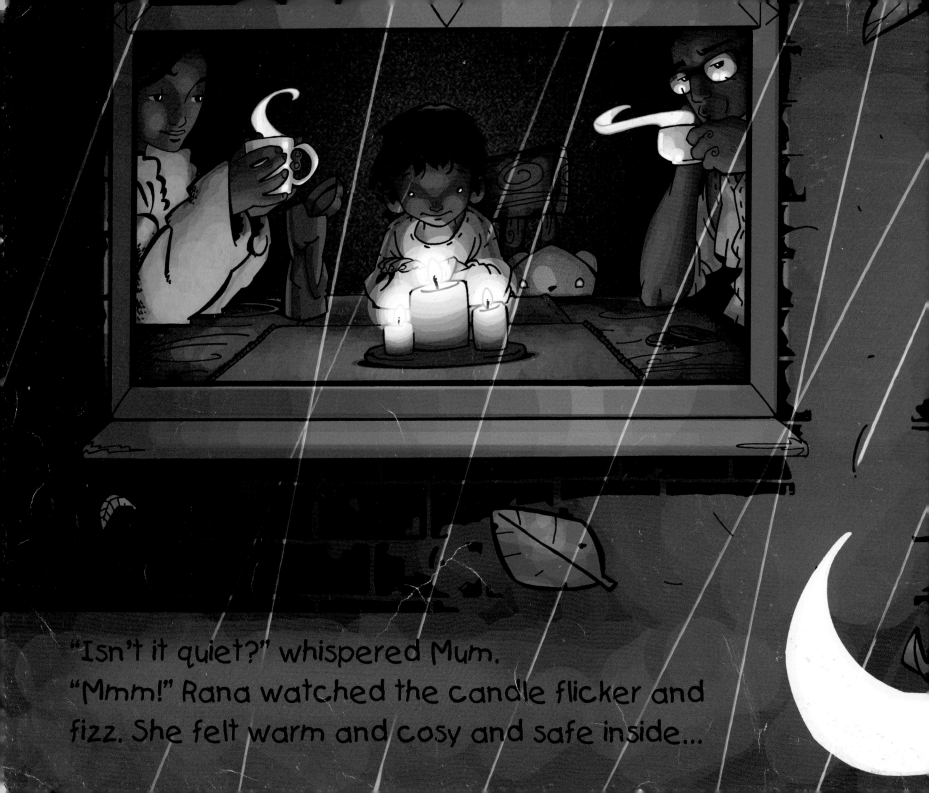

"Isn't it quiet?" whispered Mum.
"Mmm!" Rana watched the candle flicker and fizz. She felt warm and cosy and safe inside...

while the storm stamped on the trees outside.

Then Rana said, "Can me and Fluffy Bear have something to eat?"

They had a banana,
a biscuit and some milk.

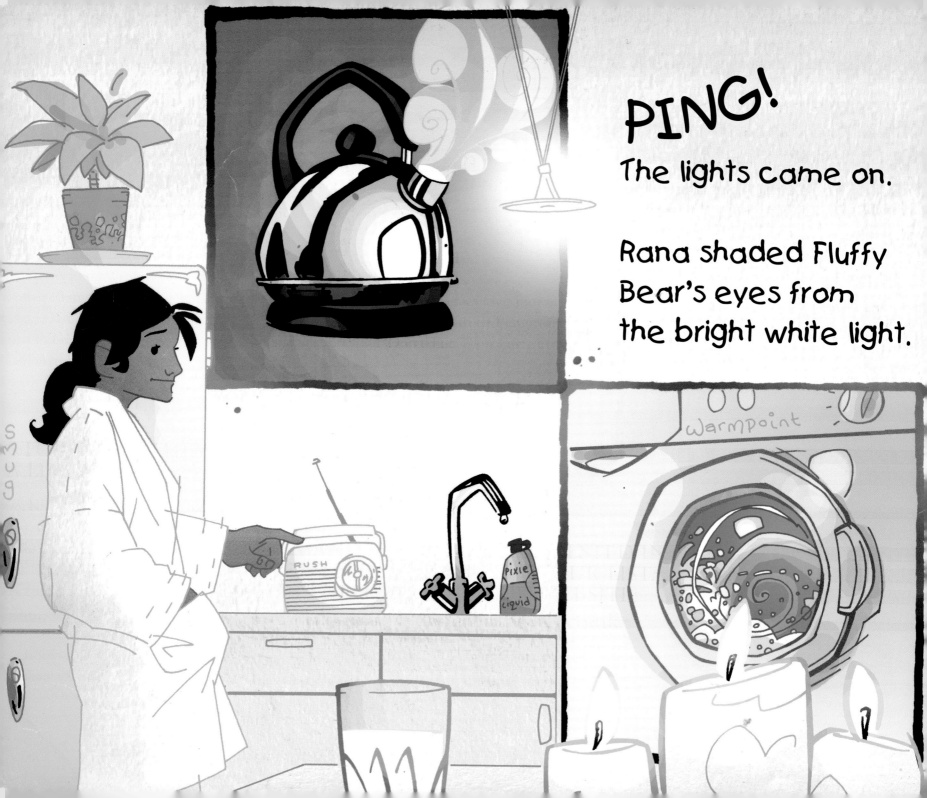

PING!

The lights came on.

Rana shaded Fluffy Bear's eyes from the bright white light.

The TV crackled.
The kettle hissed.
The washing machine
BUMP BUMP BUMPED.
"Now go to bed,
Rana!" Dad said.

Rana dragged
her feet on the stairs.
"Do I have to?
I'm not tired."
"It's way past
your bedtime," said Mum.

In the bedroom Rana missed the darkness as wide as the ocean.

Then Mum tried to switch the night light on. "Sorry, it's broken!"

"Oh no!" Rana climbed into bed. "Never mind," Mum smiled. "I'll leave the door open. The hall light's on."

"Open the door really wide," Rana begged. "You know Fluffy Bear hates the dark."

"Enough!" Mum laughed and folded her arms. "I'm going now. Night night."

"Oh, okay. Good night."

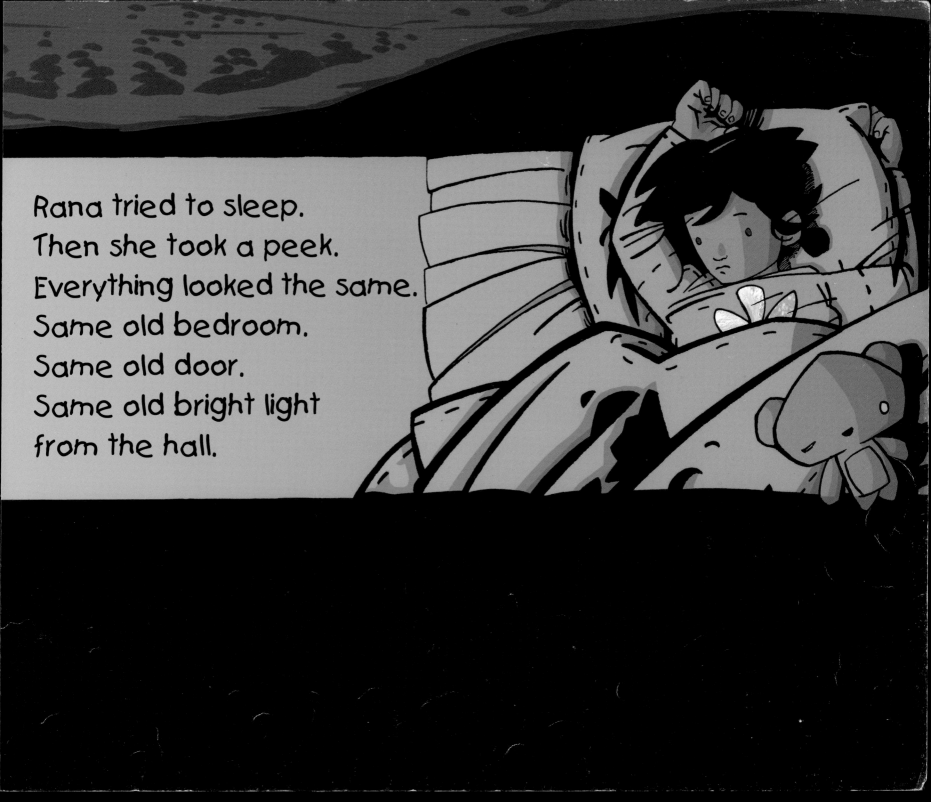

Rana tried to sleep.
Then she took a peek.
Everything looked the same.
Same old bedroom.
Same old door.
Same old bright light
from the hall.

Rana jumped out of bed and closed the door.

"That horrible light's gone now!"
She hugged Fluffy Bear tight.

Rana fell asleep
in a darkness as wide as the ocean.

Published by Tamarind Ltd, 2006
PO Box 52
Northwood
Middx HA6 1UN

Text © Anna Perera
Illustrations © Carl Pearce
Edited by Simona Sideri

ISBN 1 870516 77 X

Printed in Singapore

OTHER TAMARIND TITLES

FOR *The Night the Lights Went Out* READERS

What Will I Be?

All My Friends

A Safe Place

Dave and the Tooth Fairy

Where's Gran?

Time for Bed

Time to Get Up

Giant Hiccups

Are We There Yet?

Mum's Late

BOOKS FOR WHEN THEY GET A LITTLE OLDER...

Princess Katrina and the Hair Charmer

Caribbean Animals

The Feather

The Bush

Marty Monster

Starlight

Dizzy's Walk

Boots for a Bridesmaid

Yohance and the Dinosaurs

FOR TODDLERS

The Best Blanket

The Best Home

The Best Mum

The Best Toy

Let's Feed the Ducks

Let's Go to Bed

Let's Have Fun

Let's Go to Playgroup

I Don't Eat Toothpaste Anymore

FOR BABIES

Baby Goes

Baby Plays

Baby Noises

Baby Finds

AND IF YOU ARE INTERESTED IN SEEING THE REST OF OUR LIST, PLEASE VISIT OUR WEBSITE:

www.tamarindbooks.co.uk